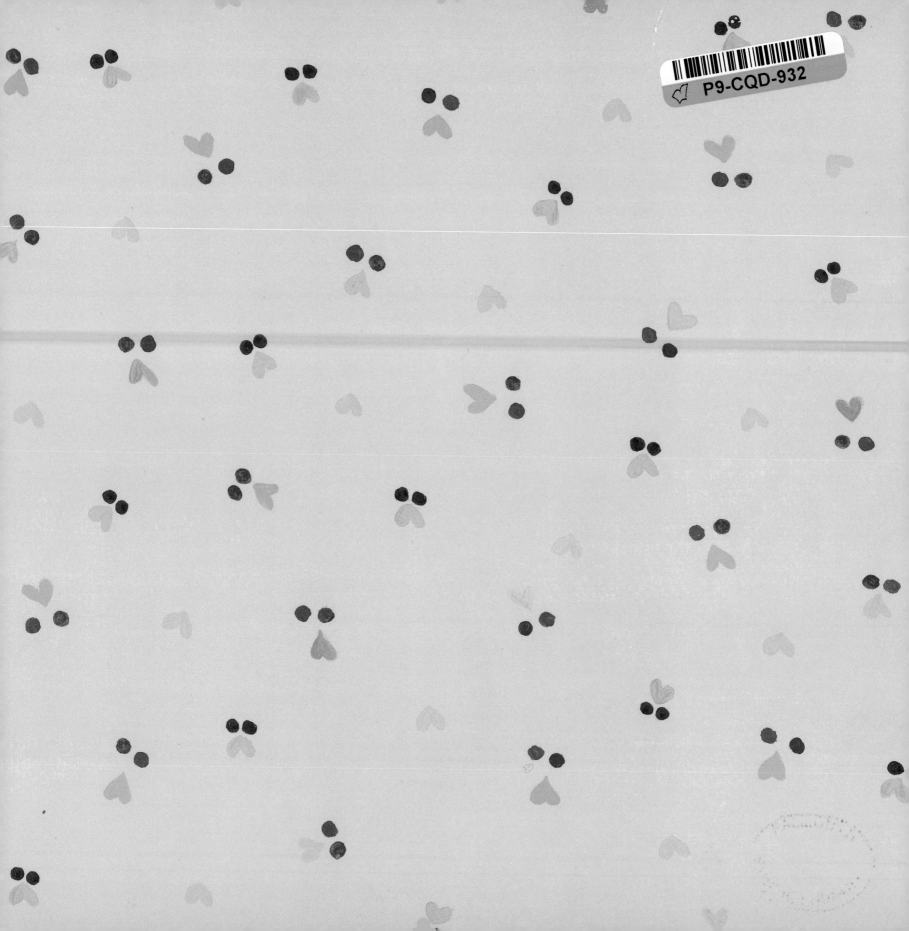

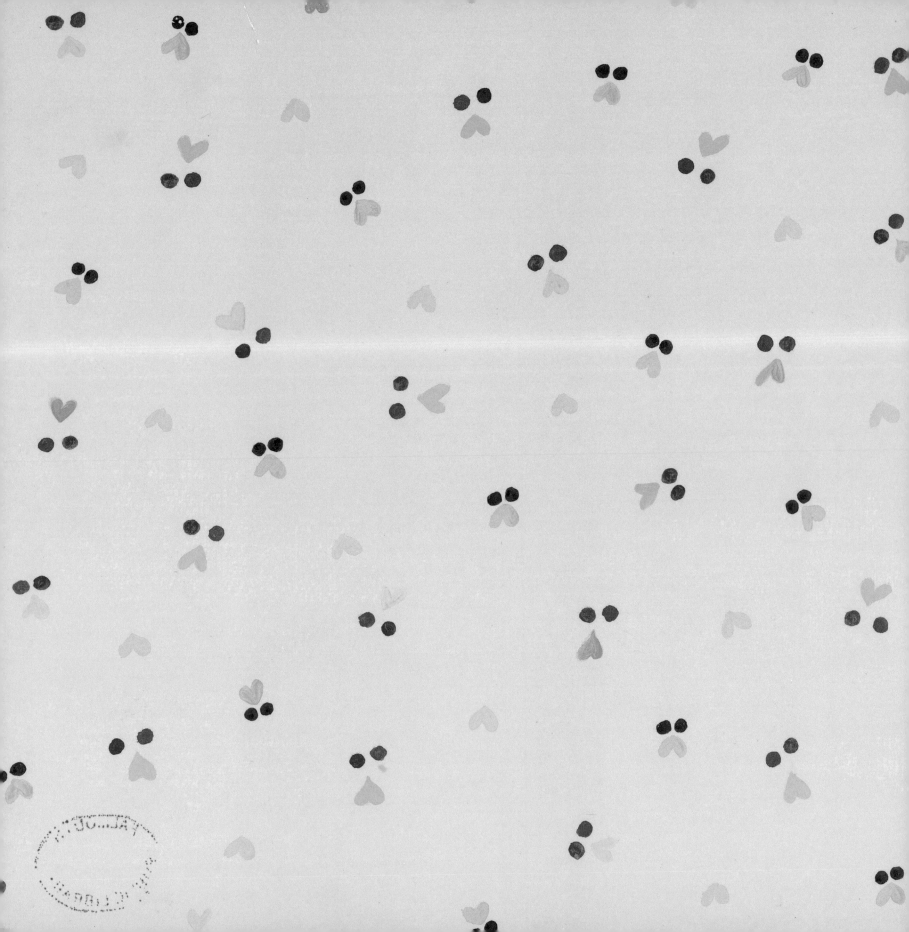

Here We Go Round the Mulberry Bush

Sophie Fatus & Fred Penner

Barefoot Books
Celebrating Art and Story

Here we go round the mulberry bush,
the mulberry bush, the mulberry bush.

Here we go round the mulberry bush,
early in the morning.

This is the way we jump out of bed,
jump out of bed, jump out of bed.

This is the way we jump out of bed,
early in the morning.

This is the way we wash ourselves,
wash ourselves, wash ourselves.

This is the way we wash ourselves,
early in the morning.

This is the way we brush our teeth,

brush our teeth, brush our teeth.

This is the way we brush our teeth,
early in the morning.

This is the way we comb our hair,
comb our hair, comb our hair.

This is the way we comb our hair,
early in the morning.

This is the way we put on our clothes,
put on our clothes, put on our clothes.

This is the way we put on our clothes,
early in the morning.

This is the way we eat our food,
eat our food, eat our food.

This is the way we eat our food,
early in the morning.

This is the way we clean our bowls,
clean our bowls, clean our bowls.

This is the way we clean our bowls

early in the morning.

This is the way we go to school,
go to school, go to school.

This is the way we go to school,
early in the morning.

This is the way we wave good-bye,
wave good-bye, wave good-bye.

This the way we wave good-bye,

good-bye, khanbiafo, namaste, joi gin

early in the morning!

Here We Go Round the Mulberry Bush

Here we go round the mul-ber-ry bush, the mul-ber-ry bush, the

mul-ber-ry bush. Here we go round the mul-ber-ry bush, ear-ly in the mor-ning.

This is the way we jump out of bed . . .

This is the way we wash ourselves . . .

This is the way we brush our teeth . . .

This is the way we comb our hair . . .

This is the way we put on our clothes . . .

This is the way we eat our food . . .

This is the way we clean our bowls . . .

This is the way we go to school . . .

This is the way we wave good-bye . . .

Early in the morning!

The Song

"Here We Go Round the Mulberry Bush" is a traditional song that has been around for hundreds of years. There are lots of stories about where it came from.

In some versions of the story, a mulberry bush is said to keep people safe. Joining hands in a circle and dancing to the right keeps evil fairies away. In other versions, the game was created by a washerwoman, so her children could play nearby while she worked. She made up a rhyme and dance about the mulberry bush in her yard. In the Celtic tradition, during country weddings, known as *rush weddings*, it was common to dance around a mulberry bush.

Whichever the story, a fun fact is that mulberries grow on trees, not bushes! The trees have heart-shaped leaves and grow red fruit on their branches.

The Dance

There is a fun dancing game that goes along with this song. Everyone holds hands and starts to sing and dance or skip around in a circle. For each verse, everyone stops to do what the song says. When you sing this verse:

"This is the way we brush our teeth, brush our teeth, brush our teeth. This is the way we brush our teeth, early in the morning."

. . . you pretend that you are brushing your teeth. You can even make up your own verses as you go along!

For my precious friend Dona — S. F.

Barefoot Books
124 Walcot Street
Bath BA1 5BG, UK

Barefoot Books
2067 Massachusetts Ave
Cambridge, MA 02140, USA

First published in Great Britain by Barefoot Books, Ltd and in
the United States of America by Barefoot Books, Inc in 2007

Graphic design by Louise Millar, London
Reproduction by Grafiscan, Verona
Printed and bound in Singapore by Tien Wah Press

Library of Congress Cataloging-in-Publication Data
Fatus, Sophie.
    Here we go round the mulberry bush / Sophie Fatus.
        p. cm.
    Summary: Presents ten verses of the popular song, with illustrations
of children from different cultures as they get ready for school.
    ISBN-13: 978-1-84686-035-5 (hardcover : alk. paper)
    1. Children's songs, English--United States--Texts.   [1. Morning
--Songs and music. 2. Songs.]   I. Title.
    PZ8.3.F2345Her 2007
    782.42--dc22
    [E]

                                2006025656

British Cataloguing-in-Publication Data:
a catalogue record for this book is available from the British Library

                        3 5 7 9 8 6 4 2

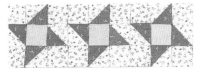

Night came, and Selina crawled into her bed in her small room upstairs. "What a lovely day. Now if only Father would come home," she murmured to herself. She was almost asleep when she finally heard his horse and buggy coming up the lane. She could just make out the sound of Mother lifting the door latch and hurrying out to meet him.

Father's deep voice drifted through Selina's open window. He spoke firmly to Mother. "We must move to Upper Canada within the month, Annie. War is coming. Soldiers are killing each other by the thousands." He paused to take a deep breath. "Uncle Jacob told me that in Virginia the armies of the South are already saying our people are disloyal. Mennonite property and farmlands are being destroyed. Many of our meeting houses have been burned to the ground."

Mother's sobs shook Selina to the core. Father continued talking in a softer voice. "We can go to Upper Canada. There is work for me at the sawmill of Jacob Snyder. I can save money to buy farmland. It is rich and fertile . . ."

Selina tried to listen further, but soon fell into a troubled sleep filled with dreams of fighting and gunfire.

In the morning Selina raced downstairs and into her father's arms. He still wore his charcoal Sunday suit with the turned-up collar. His eyes were tired, as though he had not slept.

"Is it true, Father," Selina asked, "that we will have to leave our farm? Is war coming?"

"Yes, it is true that we will have to move," he answered wearily. "There is no place for us in a country that is at war. But there will be many relatives and friends for you, Selina, in Upper Canada."

Days of hurried packing followed. There was talk about the train they would ride, with its smoking, wood-burning locomotive.

On some days the excitement bubbled inside Selina when she thought of chugging across the distant land on iron rails. But at other times she was almost overwhelmed with sadness, for Grandmother would be staying behind.

"Selina, I will not go along with you to Upper Canada," Grandmother had explained. "I am old now, too old to start my life again. I'll stay here in Pennsylvania with my brother Noah and his family."

On the day before they were to leave, Grandmother called Selina into the kitchen. "Come, child," she said. "Let's spread out the new quilt top. It's almost finished."

Before them unfolded the warm, bright beauty of the matching pieces of cloth that held memories for everyone in their family.

"I am giving this quilt top to you, Selina. Take it to your new home, and when it is quilted, spread it out over your bed. You will think of me whenever you look at it."

Selina hugged the precious gift tightly in her arms.

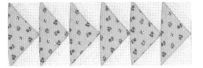

A large farm wagon with a four-horse team came the next day to carry Selina and her family to the train station in Lancaster.

There was the locomotive, hissing with steam. Soon the train was rolling through the countryside. The next afternoon the train came to the suspension bridge that crossed the Niagara River into Upper Canada. Thin webs of iron swung perilously through the sky, connecting one country with another. Far down in the gorge, the river churned in rushing whirlpools.

It seemed an eternity before the train finally stopped in Berlin, near Waterloo, where Selina and her family would live. Through the window Selina saw a horse-drawn farm wagon just like the ones at home.

"It's Uncle Isaac Eby!" Father cried, jumping up to greet him.

Uncle Isaac, in his homespun farm clothes, laughed and shook their hands. "You will stay with us until your new house is ready," he said as he led them away.

Aunt Minerva met them at the door, her hands folded over a starched white apron and her smooth brown hair tucked neatly under her head covering. She bent down to take Selina's quilt top from her arms.

"Oh, no." Selina drew back. "It's my quilt top from Grandmother."

"Quilt top!" The four Eby daughters suddenly appeared at the open front door. "Let's spread it out on top of the kitchen table."

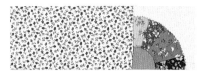

The dark green patches from Grandmother's wedding dress and the flowered daisies from Selina's baby clothes and the many, many squares of memory shone strong and beautiful in the sunny kitchen.

"It's the Bear Paw pattern," Selina told them, thinking of Grandmother as she traced the pattern with her fingertips.

"In Canada we call this pattern Duck's Foot in the Mud," one of her cousins said, laughing. "It came to us here from our English neighbors."

"We'll have a quilting bee soon for Selina's quilt top," Aunt Minerva announced. "And we can order a bolt of flowered red cambric for the backing."

Selina smiled. "I would like the quilt for my bed in our new house when it is finished."

"Of course," everyone agreed.

That night, when Selina went up to the bedroom where her four cousins slept, she found a Log Cabin quilt on her bed.

"Look, Selina," her oldest cousin, Clara, said. "The quilt on your bed has patches on it from all four of our Sunday dresses. Mother says the pattern jumps around just the way we do."

Selina's heart was so heavy with missing home that at first she barely glanced at the quilt. Then suddenly she gasped. "I see a patch that came from Grandmother's wedding dress!"

"Of course, Selina," Clara said, pointing to the many scattered dark green squares of cloth. "Your grandmother gave the pieces to our mother."

A soft summer wind blew through the open window, bearing with it the scent of the wheat and barley growing in the fields. Selina smiled at the memory of her grandmother, knowing she would always be with her, and there was peace in her heart.